Jimmathy's Odyssey

3

A Tale of Likely Heroes

Violet Alton
Elsie Schwarz
Simon Sidorski
Isaac Tenholder

Emily Wilson, Editor

En Route Books and Media, LLC
Saint Louis, MO

⊛ENROUTE
Make the time

En Route Books and Media, LLC
5705 Rhodes Avenue
St. Louis, MO 63109

Contact us at
contact@enroutebooksandmedia.com

Cover Credit: Violet Alton, Elsie Schwarz, Simon Sidorski, Isaac Tenholder, and Emily Wilson

© 2025 Violet Alton, Elsie Schwarz, Simon Sidorski, Isaac Tenholder, and Emily Wilson

ISBN-13: 979-8-88870-437-0
Library of Congress Control Number:
Available online at https://catalog.loc.gov

Dedicated to all the Jimmathy's of the World

(and to anyone else who bothered to read this page)

Acknowledgments

We thank Emily Wilson for the great edits she made, and our teachers Mrs. Trudell and Mrs. Eaton for encouraging us along the way. As our hero Jimmathy's world continues to grow, we thank every person who gets the first, second, and this Jimmathy book. And finally, we thank any and every person who is a Jimmathy at heart. We love writing from Jimmathy's point of view, so we all hope it makes you all smile.

-The Jimmathers,
Elsie S, Simon S, Isaac T, Violet A, and Emily W.

Notice

Hello. We would like to add this note as a friendly reminder that the *Jimmathy's Odyssey* quintilogy is a <u>*fictional story*</u>. This means rules that apply in this story may not necessarily apply in real life. This means:

A. In real life, we would not recommend running across the ocean as a means of travel. Jimmathy Davis is a trained professional water sprinter, and, more importantly, a fictional character. If you try to do this, you will likely sink. Or worse.

B. In real life, rhinos are not evil. They are in fact, herbivores, and an endangered species. In real life, we should be helping rhinos, not fighting them over jack-hammers.

C. Reliance on goblins appearing and granting you wishes is not a wise plan.

D. Over nine in ten doctors agree that eating dirt pickles is hazardous to your health.

E. Most doctors also agree that you should wash your hands more than once every 14 years.

These facts are important to remember when reading Jimmathy. But the most important piece of information may well be:

F. Just use your common sense, man!

Table of Contents

Chapter 1

Diamond-sions, Professor Rupert, and Tahlia the Non-Squoosh

If you've read *Jimmathy's Odyssey 2: A Tale of Possible Heroes*, you'll know that when we last saw our hero Jimmathy, he had just been hanging off a giant volcano. He met Pierre, a kind sheep (who fell into a volcano), Drew, a human, (enough said), and became enemies with his dad, Paul, and his former BFF, Rupert. If you have not read that book, you should put this book down and read that one, even though we basically spoiled the whole thing.

Jimmathy began his descent into the deep smoky lava. But then he involuntarily turned the diamond around and held it up to the light. Several streams of bright orange light launched out in different directions. They bounced off the sides of the volcano and came back together at the bottom. Suddenly, the diamond began to grow and grow until it was Jimmathy size. Jimmathy suddenly felt a magnetic pull. It pulled him closer and closer, and then, suddenly, he got sucked in the diamond!

For a moment, all he could see was swirling orange clouds whooshing past him. Suddenly, the diamond spit him out and Jimmathy fell onto solid ground. He stood up and looked around. He wasn't falling into the volcano anymore, that was for sure. He looked down. The ground was soft and squishy. Everything was. It was as if he was in a dimension made of Squooshmellow, a super-squishy stuffed animal brand. Whenever you squished them, they went *"sQoOsH"*!

"Hello!" A voice called from a distance. Several living Squooshmellows appeared out of the squishy bushes. "My name's Sawtelle!"

"And my name is Natnat!" said a rabbitish creature.

"And mine's Rolnalda!" said a yeti. Jimmathy waved to them and saw something crazy.

"I'm Gideon," said a bowl of guacamole. Then, Gideon flipped himself inside out and said, "and I'm Austin!" Said an avocado.

Jimmathy was surprised. Where was he? Where was Pierre? And Rupert? As much as he was mad at Rupert for trading him for his job, he also missed Rupert's kind face. It was his goal to be friends again.

"Hi..." Jimmathy said. He hid

the diamond in his back pocket. "Have any snacks?"

The Sqooshmellows looked around. "I don't know if we have the kind of food you eat in The Space Diamond-sion, but..." said Rolnalda as she scratched her head. "Maybe Tahlia would have some human food." The other Squooshmellows nodded in agreement.

"Maybe." Austin said. Then he flipped himself inside out and Gideon came out.

"Let's go!" The Squooshmellows formed a line and marched off. Jimmathy, figuring they knew what they were doing, marched behind them. It was awfully hard to march on ground made of squooshy, but Jimmathy kept going. SQUOOSH! SQUOOSH! SQUOOSH! Every step he took gave a satisfying squoosh. Jimmathy squooshed all the way to a large squooshy house. The squoosh mailbox read, *Tahlia Choi the Non-Squoosh.*

Jimmathy's eyes widened. He remembered Tahlia from a few weeks ago—maybe 5 or 6. It was weird because he usually forgot people that he knew. One time, he actually forgot who Rupert was! His stomach felt jittery. He was very hungry.

"Here?" Jimmathy asked. Suddenly, he couldn't move.

"Uh, yeah," Natnat said. She pushed open a door in the fence. They walked into a beautiful garden. Several Squooshmellow garden gnomes watered and planted plants and squooshy beanstalks in the flower beds. A small cottage with fake smoke coming out of the chimney sat in the middle of the mess.

"Yes, yes, over here." Sawtelle led

the way. Jimmathy felt jittery and more jittery with each squooshy step to the cottage. Was his stomach grumbling too much? Or was it something else?

If you're wondering why Jimmathy is acting up, it's because of the pear that he got from Tahlia's parents. He wasn't sure what to say about it... or the whole mess at all. Jimmathy reached for the door. He touched it with his fingertips but then recoiled.

"Well, open it already." said Sawtelle.

Jimmathy stopped. He opened it, shivering and trembling. "Tail-a?" He hollered.

"Who's Tail-a?" asked Austin. Suddenly, they heard a creak in the floor. A beautiful young woman with shiny black hair walked over. She had light brown skin and wore a

Squooshmellow-sponsored shirt.

"Jimmathy?" She shrugged. "I didn't know you lived here!"

"Well, I don't... Long story. Have any food?"

Tahlia shrugged. "I was expecting you to be still eating off that pear you stole from my umma and appa. I think I have some cereal in here."

If you are wondering where all the things that have been used for the quests are, once the spell works, they get zapped off to where the Questee found them. So, really, Jimmathy could go back to North Korea and get the pear again. But Jimmathy didn't like pears.

"Uhhhh.... Cereal's fine." Jimmathy invited himself inside and somehow found the cereal in one of the wooden cabinets. He could sniff food out—if he was very desperate for it—anywhere.

"So, what brings you here to the Squooshmellow Diamond-sion?" Tahlia asked. She sat herself on one of the chairs and sipped her tea. Jimmathy ate his cereal at the small kitchen table.

"What?! I'm in the Squooshmellow Diamond-sion? What is that? How did I get here?"

Tahlia sighed and took a long sip of tea, then pushed her glasses up her nose and began. "We are in the Squooshmellow Diamond-sion. By 'Diamond-sion', we mean a different dimension where how you get here is by using a Diamond. *This* diamond-sion is made entirely out of Squooshmellow, that popular, squishy, stuffed animal. I'm guessing you got here by your Diamond."

"Huh?"

Tahlia paused. "Jimmathy, what happened right before you got blasted here?"

Jimmathy thought about it. "Um... I was hanging by a volcano. I slipped and fell in, but luckily my friend sheep threw me a... Oh! A diamond!"

"Gotcha." said Tahlia. "Okay. So your sheep friend made that Diamond out of your three favourite things. I know this is all very new right now. But you'll learn more. Oh yeah, one more thing: Don't think you want to stay. It gets boring. In fact, you want to get *out of here*. I miss TSD."

"TSD?"

"It's short for 'The Space Diamond-sion'. That is where you and I are from!"

"Oh."

"So... How did you end up here?" Tahlia asked.

Jimmathy replied, "volcanoes....

Grey-faced rats.... Stupid betraying friends. I didn't know YOU lived here."

"My umma and appa used to have a farm in North Korea, but they moved to South Korea last month. I live here. I knew about changing diamond-sions since I was a little kid. My grandma lived here, too. You know," she gestured to the diamond that Jimmathy set on the table, "A diamond is the only way to change diamond-sions."

"So?" said Jimmathy, his mouth full of milk and Delishi-O's.

"I don't have a Diamond. I'm stuck here." Tahlia sighed.

"But didn't I see you at that one school?" asked Jimmathy. He only remembered that because of the pear.

It was clear—without her he wouldn't have gotten that pear in the first place.

"Yes, yes. I suppose," she refilled her tea. "I know it doesn't make sense now, and I can't really tell you."

***

In the normal diamond-sion called The Space Dimension (more known as TSD), Drew was devastated over Pierre. He sat there crying into the volcano.

"Oh, my favourite sheep!" he wailed. "He was my favourite sheep!"

Pierre had tried to throw Jimmathy the diamond and ended up falling in. It was devastating, sure, but luckily a couple minutes after Jimmathy disappeared, Pierre flew up out of the volcano. He was a little blurry for a second but then returned to normal form.

"PIERRE!!" Drew yelled, frantically

wrapping his arms around the sheep.

"Bahhhhhh! Bahhh Bahhhhh Bah Bahh Baaa Bahhh Baaa Bah!" Pierre said in Sheepish. (Translation: "I'm fine! Sheep have twelve lives!")

"Bahhh!!" Drew exclaimed. (Translation: "Oh, yeah!")

"Where's Jimmathy?" Pierre asked in Sheepish. "Did he get the Diamond? What about Rhino, Gob-Hob, Rupert, and that smelly gulf guy? What's his name? ...Paul?"

Drew shrugged. "All I know is Jimmathy caught that diamond thing. He got blasted off somewhere. You seem pretty chill about it, so I won't ask what exactly happened there. Once you were gone, I started wailing, so I didn't see where the losers went. Prob' to WAGGA, and Paul probably went back to his house, wherever that is."

Pierre nodded. He was learning quite a bit of English and managed to say: "And so we go to WAGGA."

***

Jimmathy, meanwhile, was having the time of his life at Tahlia's. He jumped on her Squooshmellow trampoline, rolled around in Squooshmellow, and enjoyed the sunshine! It was always sunny and warm in the Squooshmellow diamond-sion. It sure was fun, but Jimmathy longed for Rupert. He wished Rupert could enjoy the things that he was doing. Jimmathy wondered what Rupert was doing right now—maybe at WAGGA doing paperwork or something like that.

But what Rupert was actually doing was sitting in GobHob's office. Usually, if you were in there it was for something very bad. In fact, it brought back bad memories of getting fired just a few months before. But really it was the opposite to Rupert in this case. Rupert had known about this secret for a few days now but never thought it would be for real.

Rupert knew that if anything like this would ever happen, he would tell Jimmathy first thing. But he did not. They were now pure enemies, and Rupert felt *really*, *REALLY* bad about the whole trading thing. In fact, it was because of them breaking up as friends that this actually happened...

Long story.

In short, Rupert traded Jimmathy for his job. Jimmathy got really mad, and they weren't friends anymore. Meanwhile, GobHob was getting old and wanted to retire, so someone had to take his place. And he knew who.

Yes. Rupert was gonna be head of WAGGA.

"Well, Rupert," GobHob said, "It's gotta happen sometime, and now's as good as any."

"I suppose you're right," Rupert said. He was about to become the world leader of WAGGA. Two months ago, with Jimmathy, this would've been beyond his wildest dreams. So why didn't it feel good? GobHob removed the tan pin that read, "WAGGA Official World Leader", from his blazer and placed it on Rupert.

"Boss, I..."

"Everyone will call *YOU* Boss now."

"Okay... *Former* Boss... Umm..."

"What?"

"Uh... where's Jimmathy?" He

knew better than to talk about Jimmathy in front of GobHob, but Rupert was desperate.

GobHob laughed.

"You didn't know?!! Me and Rhino dangled him by the edge of a volcano, that's where! Dropped him in, too. Long gone. Now he's nothing more than a chunk of plaster dipped in hot sauce. That old sheep, too. Doesn't matter."

GobHob was laughing, so Rupert laughed, too.

"What actually happened, former professor?"

"You think I'm *lying* to you? Rup? You think I'm making all this things up?"

Rupert lowered his head in shame.

"No, Gob." He wondered if it was true. He hoped—no, wished on a star that GobHob was making all this up.

"I'm movin' into WAGGA Retirement Home in West Africa, if ya
need me." He closed an overly large
leather suitcase. He adjusted his
old-timey brown glasses and trotted
along a long path with a sign saying
"Path to GobHob Airlines."

Rupert sat at his new desk.

"Yep... Living the dream... *Sigh*,"
Rupert muttered so only he could
hear it. There was nobody around to
hear it anyway.

He had gone from the very bottom to the Tippy-tippy-tippy-tippy-
tippy-top in thirty seconds. But
something still felt... *Empty*. Immediately, he ran to the closest home
improvement store and bought
tons of plants and decor. He loaded
them into a truck and drove back to
WAGGA.

The decor included a small white

desk, about 17 different fake plants (Rupert hated plant care but loved plants themselves), a frame and picture of him and Jimmathy when they visited the beach three weeks ago, a small lamp, and three chairs: One to sit at on the opposite side of his desk if Rupert had to give them "the talk," one to just be comfy and decoration, and one for Rupert himself. GobHob's was not his style. Then Rupert ran to the nearest office store and stocked up on erasers, pens, pencils, office paper, paper and binder clips, scissors, highlighters, folders and binders, and felt-tip markers.

Of course, WAGGA uses Waggcoins instead of pounds or dollars, so he had to change his Waggcoins into Tuvaluan dollars. After he was satisfied with the decor and necessary supplies, he got a grey carpet.

He was almost out of money, so then, for his final item, Rupert got out a small trophy. He didn't buy it, but he earned it years ago when he won "Goblin of the Year."

His office was complete. Rupert was very pleased. He knew Jim-mathy would like it. Oh, how he missed Jimmathy. But in his heart... He knew he was long gone.

***

Jimmathy missed Rupert, too. Soon it became clear that his one mission was to get back home. And not alone. He would bring Tahlia home too. She missed her family like Jimmathy—Rupert was basically family now.

"Is there some way to get back to Rupert's diamond-sion?" Jimmathy asked. They sat in a circle in the garden—Tahlia, Jimmathy, Sawtelle, Natnat, Rolnalda, and Gideon/Austin.

Tahlia started to look uncomfortable. "No, kind of, maybe... It's not important."

"Didn't you tell us once that you had a diamond?" asked Austin.

"Well, yes," Tahlia started, "usually if you have a Diamond then you can get back to TSD, but... I kind of don't have mine anymore."

They all gasped, including Jimmathy, although he didn't understand what Tahlia was saying. "What happened?" Rolnalda asked.

"I was holding onto it, and then I dropped it and lost it in the Squooshmellow fluff. I was looking around for it when *CRUNCH*—I accidentally stepped on it." Tahlia was obviously embarrassed. Hearing this, Jimmathy realised he didn't know where his diamond was currently. Last time he checked, it was in his back pocket. But it must have slipped out when he was trampolining.

"Holly nutcrackers!" Jimmathy cried. "I can't find mine either!"

There was a long period of silence.

"You know we both need diamonds to get out of here, right?" Tahlia asked.

"It's alright, we can retrace our steps," Natnat said.

And so they did—or tried anyway.

"I don't see why we should be looking for this." Tahlia complained. "I also need a diamond if I'm gonna get out of here. Diamonds are made of three of your favourite (non-living) things. My things are long gone, and so is my Diamond."

"But no one knows if the things to make a diamond disappear or go to some special place after you make yours," Rolnalda pointed out. "Your things could be someplace special, we just don't know."

"Same with Jimmathy," Natnat sighed. They didn't know what to do.

"But if that place DOES exist, we're gonna find it!" Gideon announced.

"We will!" Austin said after Gideon flipped himself inside out to show Austin.

"So... let's map out the most likely locations of this so-called 'Item Cave,'" Tahlia said while pulling out a map.

"We're a million billion trillion quadrillion jillion bazillion quintillion gazillion times lucky if it happens to be in *this* diamond-sion," groaned Rolnalda.

"What!?!?" exclaimed Jimmathy. "I mean, how many diamond-sions can there be, anyway?"

"Around Infinite. There are seven thousand, eight hundred and ninety-nine to the fifth power to be exact... although we're still counting. Odds are, yes, there are infinities," said Sawtelle.

"So let me get this straight: There's an infinity-minus-one percent chance that we can't find the Diamond... without a Diamond," said Jimmathy.

"Yep, pretty much," sighed Natnat.

"Since you clearly don't know how to operate a Diamond, you're just lucky that your diamond didn't drop you off in the constantly raining fire dimension. The weather there is terrible," Tahlia said.

"It's constantly raining fire," said

Austin.

"Would not recommend," said Rolnalda.

"Wait, you said seven thousand, eight hundred and ninety-nine to the fifth power, right?" Jimmathy asked.

"Yup, at least." Tahlia responded.

"I have no idea what powers are, but seven thousand, eight hundred and ninety-nine is small compared to gazillion, the largest number I can think of," Jimmathy said, "we would need 20,911 more to get to gazillion.

"How!?!?" Austin exclaimed.

"I don't know, it just came to me," Jimmathy said.

"I have an idea!" Tahlia jumped up. "We find someone else's Diamond and use it to travel instead!" All the Squooshmellows looked at Tahlia suspiciously.

"Uh, no way," Natnat said, "you

have to use your own. You'll get in HUMONGOUS trouble."

The other Squooshmellows nodded. Jimmathy shrugged as if to say, "Sorry, I guess they're right".

Tahlia slumped down. They were out of ideas, and Jimmathy was scared he would be stuck here forever.

***

Drew and Pierre bolted to WAGGA World HQ. They asked a friendly looking goblin—she had red hair that exploded out of her head—where Rupert was.

"Do I know you?" the goblin asked, which was not answering their question.

Drew froze. This was the guard who had locked them into their cell in WAGGA jail. They had escaped. It had been two days since then. Drew frantically stammered, "uh—no. No no no no. Nope you don't. I should be getting on my day now, so-"

"YOU!" The guard burst. Drew and Pierre tried to run, but it was too late. She already had handcuffs on Drew and multiple rubber bands and paperclips on Pierre's hooves. (Because handcuffs don't fit on sheep).

"Please," Pierre bleated, "we're here to see Rupert and GobHob." But the guard didn't speak Sheep-ish, so it was no use. Pierre tried to speak in English the best he could. "Baaaplebse." —Drew glared at Pierre— "Beher baaaacaase baaa... BUPERT baaaa baa ba?"

Suddenly, Rupert opened the door to WAGGA World HQ. Rupert peered over and noticed Drew and Pierre and quickly ran over.

"Betsie! Please let them go! In one week I am gonna be the head of WAGGA. It is my order. LET. THEM. GO."

Betsie—apparently the guard's name—sighed but let them go. Rupert did that because he recognised Pierre from when they were at Paul's house and Drew from when he stumbled into the jail a few days ago. But also Rupert knew they were Jimmathy's friends, and he knew that Jimmathy would appreciate that.

That was really all he could do for Jimmathy now. Rupert took Drew and Pierre into his new office.

"Jimmathy's gone," Rupert said and sniffed. Pierre and Drew sat down on one of the seats in the room.

"Baaaa!" Pierre interrupted.

"He's saying that Jimmathy

might not be gone," Drew translated. "Actually, Pierre threw Jimmathy his Diamond, one that can change dimensions, but we're not sure if we got it in time."

"I've heard of those. Diamonds, I mean." Rupert put his hand on his chin. "Let's hope he got it."

For some reason, Rupert knew that Jimmathy caught it. He knew it. But Rupert needed to prove it.

"If there was some possible way Jimmathy got that Diamond and got sucked into a different diamond-sion, the dimensions where you have to use a Diamond, then I'm gonna get my own Diamond, get sucked into a Diamond-sion, and find Jimmathy no matter what. I would go to the moon and back for him. He's the bestest friend I've ever had," Rupert said proudly.

"I don't mean to interfere, but I

think travelling to a different dimension is a bit farther than to the moon and back," said a voice in the shadows. It was GobHob. He came out of the shadows, revealing himself. GobHob smirked at his brilliant entrance.

"I thought you were already at that Nursing Home," Rupert said.

"It's WAGGA *Retirement* Home. And no, I decided at the last moment to just chicken out. Wanted to stay here for the next week to see how ya do before you become head of WAG." GobHob leaned in closer to Rupert. "But one more word about Jimmathy, I'll be taking it right back. Your 'friend' is long gone. You know that, so stop talkin' 'bout him."

GobHob paused and looked at his old office. He scowled at the homey style and fake plants.

"You know, if you wanna be head

of WAGGA, then you better act like it." GobHob said. "Put your serious face on. This isn't all fun and games, ya know. When you were young, I remember, you knew that. You knew it's all business. But when you gave Jimmathy his quest, man. It was a mess. I fired you for a reason. If you want to keep this job, you better act like it, ya understand?"

Rupert nodded. "Yes, sir." GobHob left.

GobHob didn't even notice Pierre and Drew, and that might have been a good thing. A few days ago, Jimmathy, Rupert, and Paul encountered Rhino and GobHob, and it wasn't pretty, because a *sheep* was involved. A sheep who would do anything anyone said. Of course, that would be a good thing, unless two people were fighting over it. GobHob would have been a mess if he saw Pierre again.

"We gotta get me a Diamond," Rupert whispered as soon as he was sure GobHob was gone. "Gotta get me to a different diamond-sion."

Drew and Pierre hesitated.

"Not sure that's the best idea, Rup," Drew said.

"Why? You don't want to save Jimmathy?"

"Number one, we're not sure if Jimmathy even *caught* his Diamond. Two, Pierre only gave Jimmathy his Diamond because he knew he was in serious trouble and had to get out. Travelling diamond-sions is very dangerous, and you should only do it if you are in VERY grave danger. I don't want you risking your life for nothing." Drew said cautiously.

"You sure know a lot about Diamonds," Rupert grumbled.

"Pierre taught me everything I needed to know!" Drew protested.

"Baaaa! Ba ba baaaa ba baaa…. Baa baaa ba!" Pierre bleated loudly.

"What's he saying?" Rupert asked.

"He's saying another reason you shouldn't go is that people lose their Diamonds very easily. Your Diamond is your only way in and out of Diamond-sions, so you could be stuck in there forever!"

Rupert didn't hesitate to say back, "And that's more the reason I should go! Jimmathy loses stuff ALL THE TIME, and HE more than likely lost his Diamond before he hit the ground. That means he's probably stuck there, and we need to rescue him!"

Drew and Pierre started to get a little annoyed and tired of arguing with Rupert. But suddenly Pierre remembered something. He whispered it in Drew's ear, and he translated,

"But you wouldn't *rescue* him, since he needs his *own* Diamond to get back home. And I—"

"*We're going to get me my Diamond and go find Jimmathy and find his Diamond to go home. No more arguments. THIS. IS. FINAL.*" Rupert growled, slamming his foot down on the wood.

"Then, we're not coming." Drew said.

"Okay." Rupert replied pleasantly.

Drew thought about it. "Fine, we'll come."

Chapter 2

Hyperventilating, Songs Sung Backwards, and Potion Houses

Jimmathy was, in a way, panicking. It was unlike him, Rupert would say, to hyperventilate.

"Geez, why is he acting like that?" Rolnalda asked Tahlia.

"Maybe he's having a panic attack," Austin whispered.

"Probably not," Tahlia said. She quickly ran over to Jimmathy, who was wheezing and doing the worm on the Squooshmellow ground.

Sawtelle gasped. "I know what's happening," she whispered. Tahlia quickly whipped around.

"What?"

"No time to explain. We need to

get to the nearest potion house, stat."

"*Potion* House?!" Tahlia burst.

Jimmathy started to calm down. "*Bananas eating Jackhammer Diamond Telecubes...*" he moaned.

"WHAT IS GOING ON??!!" Tahlia yelled. Rolnalda paused and bit her lip.

"Someone has stolen and broken his Diamond." She looked around nervously. "...Or found the place where Jimmathy's three favourite things are and broke or damaged them."

Tahlia and the other Squoosh-mellows gasped. Tahlia's eyes widened. "You mean that place exists?" She asked.

"It's definitely possible. All we know is it has to be something about Jimmathy's connection to the diamond-sions."

"*Why* would someone be after his three favourite things or his Diamond?" Gideon asked. The air grew tense.

"And who?" Natnat wondered. "Does Jimmathy have an arch nemesis?" There was silence.

"Maybe it was an accident." Austin wondered. "It's definitely possible."

"No, he's only acting like this if someone is *purposely* and madly doing it," Sawtelle trembled.

"This is very, very bad."

Jimmathy started to settle down, but then started to hype up again.

"Bananas! Bananas!" And then— oh no—he started to sing!

"*I went to a skatepark*
Saw a banana
I went to pick it up, but then I couldn't even bear it
Luckily, a jackhammer fell across

the street

But then a random rhino took it by its feet!

Bananas!

Oh, bananas!

Bananas make me go bananas!

Bananas!"

"STOP!!" Austin yelled, covering his ears. "Please, Sawtelle, it seems as if Jimmathy is in a trance! I can't bear it anymore."

Sawtelle sighed and put her hand on Jimmathy's shoulder. He stopped singing. "He can't help it. His body is getting pulled in all different directions. Since his connection to here is bad, his Diamond is broken, one part of him needs to get back to TSD, but one wants him to stay here in Squooshmellow. This causes him to be weird and dance and stuff," Sawtelle explained. "I told you. We need to get to the nearest potion house; it's the only way to make him better."

"I went there once," Natnat said, "It's not far, just a few minutes up the Squoosh Road."

"Alright, lead the way," Tahlia said.

"Aughhh, EoeOOGse? YaAaAaA!" Jimmathy said, curled up on the floor. Then he started laughing maniacally and his eyes rolled in opposite directions. Tahlia picked up his feet and dragged him along. Jimmathy blew a loud raspberry. "You can lead a horse to maple syrup, but you can't make him put a pancake up his nose!"

"HEY!" Sawtelle yelled. "That's offensive to pancakes!"

"A horse nose better fits a crape anyway." Said Jimmathy grumpily.

"Stay focused, everyone!" snapped Rolnalda.

"'*Stay focused, everyone,*' is just '*enoyreve, desucof yats*' spelled backwards!" Jimmathy replied.

"It doesn't matter." Rolnalda sighed.

They ended up at a large building. It was crumbling, but Squooshmellows had filled the gaps and holes with Squooshmellow fluff. It had a sign-that was falling off the building-that read, "*Po i on House*". The "t" wasn't on the sign anymore.

"POISON HOUSE???!!!!" Tahlia screeched, "Better not go in there."

Rolnalda sighed. "No, it used to say 'Potion House.' The "T" wore off. Stop hallucinating yourself."

Everyone took a quick glance at Jimmathy. Then they quickly looked away.

"Alright now, let's get him inside," Tahlia said.

"For the potion, we need three

grams of Dumbweed, a pint of Bab-bleapple juice, and the toenail clip-ping of the most deplorable, terrible, merciless beast in the universe known only as 'Lawyer,'" Rolnalda read aloud from a dusty old book.

"And to do what?" Tahlia asked.

"To stop whoever is doing the thing with Jimmathy's Diamond and get his Diamond himself after."

Suddenly, an old Squooshmellow toppled by.

"Ain't nobody findin' those things! Good luck...! *Not!*"

The old Squooshmellow was worn-out looking. It has rips in the fabric. Some were covered up by patches, but some were forgotten and the stuffing hung out. The face looked tired, and you couldn't really tell what it was supposed to be.

"Panda pooper!" Jimmathy yelled. Rolnalda glared at him.

"The sooner we get the items, the better." Sawtelle grumbled. Gideon nodded in agreement.

"I told you!" The old Squooshmellow barked. It had stopped in the doorway of the building. "You aren't gonna get those items! That's because they *don't exist!*"

"And how do you know?" Tahlia yelled back.

The old Squooshmellow sighed and threw some of his stuffing at Tahlia. Then he walked away.

There was silence. Until—

"First, we need to calm down Jimmathy." said Rolnalda.

"How?" Austin asked. "Is it also the spell-potion thingy?"

"No." Rolnalda said. "This is a different potion." She picked some things from a rack: A bottle of tan stuff, some white cubes—maybe some version of sugar cubes—and

Squooshmellow fabric. Everyone watched in awe as Rolnalda grinded up the fabric and put it in a cauldron, crushed up the 'sugar cubes,' and put it in, and then added the mysterious tan glop into the cauldron and stirred. It bubbled and fizzled into a soupy mix. Then the group searched the shelves for Dumbweed, Babbleapple juice, and the toenails of the wretched beast called 'lawyer'. The problem was, there wasn't any.

"None!?!?" Tahlia burst. "None of ANYTHING!?!?!"

"Let's just give Jimmathy the potion," said Natnat.

"You drink this," Rolnalda said as she put the potion into a cup and handed it to Jimmathy.

"Ew..." Jimmathy cried, "this is worse than that one stale baloney sandwich!"

Then he started to sing again.
"*Baloney*
Baloney
Phone me to baloney
Baloney
So disgusting
Baloney in all its
Joy-nee
If you but it between two pieces
of bread,
Then don't even let it go to your
head
If you wait to long to eat-ee
It it will, like I said:
Don't let it go to your head!
Don't even let it go between two
pieces of bread!"
But while his mouth was open for singing, Rolnalda forced the potion down Jimmathy's throat.

"Swallow, you devil!" Austin yelled. Jimmathy suddenly started to sing backwards!

"*Daerb fo seceip owt neewteb og ti tel neve t'nod!*"

Then he went back to normal. He blinked. He turned to Tahlia.

"What happened?"

"Someone's destroying the things you sent to the item cave!" Tahlia replied.

"WHAT!?!?!?!?" Jimmathy yelled. "Those items were our only hope of getting home!" Jimmathy wailed.

"We need the potion to fix them!" Rolnalda explained, "and stop whoever's doing it."

"Seeing Jimmathy's enemy list, I'm guessing the item smashing was no *whoopsie daisy,*" said Natnat.

"Rhino or GobHob!" Jimmathy yelled. "It *has* to be either of them!"

But then he thought about it for a second. "Wait, they left before Pierre threw me my Diamond. They don't know I'm here! They're convinced I'm dead. Who else could it be?!?"

"I don't know who those people are, but let's keep looking. Who else would want you trapped in the Squooshmellow dimension forever?"

"Grudge-holding curry shop owners, Albert Einstein, that one protective dinosaur mom, the list goes on."

Gideon and Natnat exchanged worried glances.

"Oof. It seems we might have a whole army of people who want you trapped here." Tahlia bit her lip. "I don't know how we're gonna pull this off."

"Step one is get out of this place," said Jimmathy.

"You don't think I've tried? Escape is impossible. Unless there's an invisible Diamond factory right next door, we're trapped here forever!" Tahlia cried.

Rolnalda silently scrubbed the remains of the potion out of the cauldron. Everyone else just stood there in that disgusting building. It was decomposing and had who-knew-what stuff on the floors. As soon as Rolnalda was done, Sawtelle raced out the door. Everyone followed.

Natnat scratched her alien head. "I just don't understand. Who would be mean enough to steal Jimmathy's Diamond? Who would hate him *that much*?"

Chapter 3

S.O.A.R, An Antarctic HQ, and Orange Swirls

Rupert was lost in a world of white. He spun around, lost in a sea where gravity didn't exist. He felt like he was floating in midair and falling fast at the same time. At first, he thought he saw Pierre or Drew, but it was just shadows. After about 10 seconds, the white started to fade away and a world around him started to form.

Okay, so why was Rupert doing this? And where was he? Well, I guess we should backtrack.

.mrof ot detras mih dnuora dlrow a dna yawa edaf ot detracts etihw eht ,sdnoces 01 tuoba retfA

.swodahs tsuj saw ti tub ,werD ro er-reiP saw eh thguoht eh tsrif tA. emit emas eht ta tsaf gnillaf dna riadim ni gnitaolf saw eh ekil tlef eH .tsixe t'ndid ytivarg erehw aes a ni tsol ,dnuora nups eH .etihw fo dlrow a ni tsol saw trepuR

(Okay, so that was a little mean, doing it all backwards. But now we'll *really* tell you.)

"Are you two sure this will work?" Asked Rupert.

"Positive," said Drew.

"Baaaaa!" Pierre bleated in agreement. Pierre had given them permission to enter S.O.A.R. HQ through a secret entrance concealed under a table in a restaurant in Italy. The tunnels were designed for someone the size of a sheep to fit through, so Pierre and Rupert got through without much difficulty. Drew, an average-sized human, not so much. Rupert was short enough to stand up in the narrow passage, but Drew had to belly crawl through tight spaces.

"MMMMMMPH!" Drew squeezed through the end of the tunnel, which led to a small room, seemingly a dead end, with an elderly sheep sitting in a rocking chair. She and Pierre had a conversation in Sheepish (the official language of sheep). We've taken the liberty of translating for you.

"Agent Pierre," said the elderly sheep.

"Yes, it's me." confirmed Pierre. The elderly sheep didn't have very good eyesight, but she had memorised the individual *smell* of every single S.O.A.R. agent.

"I caught your scent a mile away." The elderly sheep took another big whiff. "You brought someone else. A depressed goblin and a middle-aged human, I believe."

"They're with me."

"S.O.A.R. doesn't like outsiders in our HQ."

"I trust Drew and Rupert."

"Oh, very well. Just say the password, and I'll let you all in."

Pierre bleated the long and confusing super-secret password in sheepish. The password is far too long and confusing for us to translate, and it's super secret anyway.

The elderly sheep heard the password and peeled off the seemingly solid brick wall to reveal a door hidden underneath. She opened the door.

"You may enter."

And so, they stepped through, the world spinning. Of course, Pierre had gone through the portal multiple times, but Drew and Rupert were not used to it. Once the world of white and S.O.A.R started to appear, Rupert shook himself in shock, then rubbed his hands together.

"Time to do this thing," he announced.

Pierre looked around. "First, we'll need to grab your three favourite things."

Drew froze. He didn't move a muscle; they didn't even blink.

"You're saying that we came all the way to *Italy* and need to go all the way back to get Rupert's stuff?!" Drew barked.

"*What are you and Pierre saying*?" Rupert whispered to Drew. "*I don't speak Sheepish.*"

"He's *SAYING* that we came all the way here and need to go *back* to get your three favourite items." Drew grunted.

Pierre didn't know what Drew

was saying to Rupert because he didn't speak English very well, but Pierre did know—because of the tone in Drew's voice—that it wasn't very nice. He rolled his eyes.

Silently, Drew took out a *Foreign Language Translator Headwear LXXIV* from his pocket. He placed it over Rupert's green head, pressed the *on* button and the *English* button. Then Drew said something in Sheepish.

"Baaaa baa baaaaa ba baaaah bahhhhh ba baa!"

However, Rupert didn't hear that. He heard, "My name is Drew!" Rupert managed to smile a little. It would be much easier now.

"Drew, do you think I brought you all the way here for nothing? I plan for these types of things, you know." Pierre told Drew.

"So HOW exactly is Rupert going

to get his three favourite things close by?" Drew asked with sass in his voice.

"Yeah How?!!" Rupert agreed. But it came out as, "baaa! Ba?!!" That translator could do all sorts of things.

Pierre pointed to a series of corri-dors. "Down Corridor #179, we'll find the 56th door on the left and open it. You'll see."

Drew and Rupert followed Pierre curiously. They passed corridors, specifically corridor #97, #98, #99, #100, #101, #102, #103, #104, #105, and so on. Their legs hurt as they fi-nally passed corridor #177 and #178, and then—finally—they stopped at corridor #179.

"So we go down this hallway— sorry, *corridor*?" Rupert asked in Sheepish.

"Yes." Pierre answered. "There are

a total of 68 doors in this hallway. We will find the 56th door, it will be on the left, and then we go inside."

"Great." Drew moaned. "More walking."

***

It took ten minutes of speed-walking to finally get to the 56th door. Once they had finally caught their breath, Pierre took out his keys. It was ginormous; the ring was about the size of a basketball in diameter. Drew and Rupert's eyes widened as they saw how many keys there were. Keys filled up every space on the ring. There must have been hundreds of keys!

"Now, which key is it?" Pierre asked himself. Pierre scratched his chin. "Better start trying some!"

Rupert squeezed his eyes shut.

This was taking WAY. TOO. LONG. All he wanted to do was find Jimmathy. And he still had so many steps left. How hard was it to just save his best friend?

Possibly Jimmathy didn't even catch the diamond. Rupert couldn't bear to think about that.

What if this was all for nothing?

One hundred and thirty-three keys later, Pierre fit a key into the keyhole of the 56th door in the 179th corridor. It clicked—it worked!

"It worked!!!" Drew and Rupert exclaimed together. Pierre beamed. Then he opened the door.

Rupert and Drew peered inside, not knowing what to expect. What they saw was tons of tiny squares. They were floating in midair, and it looked like each square had a tiny name on it. There must have been billions of squares!

"Well over 10 billion, to be exact," Pierre said, finishing Rupert's sentence that was in his head.

"Wow... that is a lot of squares. In fact, that's 5 billion squared, squares!" Drew claimed.

"What are they?" Rupert asked Pierre.

"Names," Pierre remarked, "names of people, animals, goblins, stuff like that."

Pierre led Drew and Rupert over to a computer in the corner.

"What's your full name?" Pierre asked Rupert. "I'm going to search for your name, and it will show me your square. If I click on it, then your three favourite things will appear."

"My full name is Rupert Allen Waggatail—oh, and I have another middle name, but nobody uses it. "The Goblin".

Pierre typed in, "Rupert Allen, The

Goblin Waggatail." A tiny square appeared on the screen. Pierre clicked on it with his mouse, and then they had to take a form.

"Birthdate?" Pierre asked.

"September 15, 1432, was when I was born," Rupert answered.

"Phone number?"

"It's (668)-789-1011."

"Email?"

"Uh... rupert@waggamail.gob."

"Great! Last question: Address?"

Rupert paused. "I used to live in an old apartment, but now at WAGGA again because I'm the new "GobHob". Try *123 WAGGA HQ St. WAGGA Town, TV or Tuvalu 1234*. Or if that doesn't work, try *345 Normal Ct. Phoney Town, NR or Notorado 5678*."

"The WAGGA one works!" Pierre exclaimed. Then, a real-life square appeared with Rupert's full name on it. Pierre clicked on it. Suddenly, a goblin of the year trophy, a fake plant, and Rupert's old too-small car tire shirt fell onto the ground.

"Voilà."

"Woah," Rupert said.

"Now all we have to do is take them to the mix room," Pierre said.

"And where is that?" Rupert asked.

"Third floor, Corridor #192, Sixty-third door on the right."

Rupert and Drew groaned.

***

"THIRD FLOOR, CORRIDOR #192, DOOR 63 ON THE RIGHT." said Rupert tiredly.

"Whoopsie!" Pierre said. "Looks like we accidentally went to Corridor #183. I read the label wrong. Oh, well! Back we go!"

Rupert's eye twitched.

Eventually, they arrived at a door. A worn label on the door read "*Mi room.*" Pierre opened the door to reveal a room full of bottles of milk.

"Oops!" said Pierre. "I guess this is the *Milk* room. So, where's that mix room? Give me a sec..." Pierre pulled out a seemingly small sheet of paper. But then the paper unfolded itself until it stretched out across half the corridor. The top of the paper read *SOAR HQ official map*. Pierre walked up and down the corridor squinting at miniscule print on the map.

"Mix room... mix room...".

"Aha!" Rupert exclaimed, pointing to a small room labelled, "Mix Chamber".

"Oh! That only happens to be a few corridors down!" Pierre exclaimed.

Drew pointed to a moving side-walk a few meters away. "It will be faster if we take that," he said. So, they got onto the moving sidewalk.

But after only a few seconds, they realised that it was only going 1 mph. That was at most half of the speed they could have jogged.

"Alright, abandon ship." Pierre groaned.

"So, just how many corridors is a *few*?"

"Fifteen... I think." Pierre esti-mated as he stepped off the moving sidewalk. "We better run if we want to get there faster."

So, Rupert held his fake plant, Pierre held the trophy, and Drew held the tire as they ran.

It didn't take them long to make it to make it to corridor #198. (There were only two more corridors on the *whole* floor).

"Uh-oh." Pierre groaned. "This is the Mix *Chamber*. We want the Mix *Room*."

"Where's that?" asked Rupert.

"Well, it just so happens to be on the *exact* perfect opposite side of the place from where we are now."

"Well, what's the difference?"

"I... Don't know. We might as well try. What big of a difference anyway? They're practically the same."

Drew didn't say a word. He was still catching his breath.

"LET'S DO IT," said Rupert immediately. And without a word, he shoved Pierre and Drew through the door. (They were very lucky that it was unlocked.)

***

Meanwhile, Rhino and GobHob met in their special hiding place.

Frederick (Rhino's cousin), and Bob-Gob (GobHob's old assistant), were their servants.

"We need my people-finder!" GobHob yelled to Rhino. He and Rhino were sitting on large 24 karat gold thrones. They were getting served fancy food and apple juice by their RhiHob servants (RhiHob is their names put together). Their secret hideout was in Antarctica, where they were sure no one would find them. It was very cold there, but luckily they bought 73 heaters to warm their bottoms.

"Yes," Rhino said simply. He was working to speak English all the time and not slip into different languages.

"BobGob, go grab my People-Finder LXXXII. I believe it is in the closet by the front door."

BobGob hurried away.

Frederick served Rhino more bush and shrub.

GobHob looked at a newspaper.

A few minutes later, BobGob came back into the throne room carrying a rectangular device.

"Here you go, Professor Gob-Hob—I mean—King GobHob," Bob-Hob sputtered.

GobHob grudgingly took the ipad. Rhino leaned over to watch. GobHob typed in Jimmathy. His location showed up as non-existent.

"So, he *is* dead?" Rhino asked GobHob.

"Most likely, Martin."

"What about that ol' shrimp Rupert? Didn't you tell me he believes that Jimmathy is in a different dimension?" Rhino asked. GobHob typed in Rupert's name, and it showed that he was in Italy at an

Italian restaurant (or just a restaurant, since he's in Italy).

"Yes! We go there!" Rhino exclaimed, pulling out the newest-version Telecube.

"Hold up, let him cook," GobHob said, "We must surprise him."

"Costumes?-"

"NO   COSTUMES." GobHob growled. "We must be only us, acting like we are customers at the restaurant, *then* attack. We must confuse Little Rup."

"So that he thinks we're only there for fun? Okay! I could dress up as a human—"

"STOP IT WITH THE HUMAN STUFF!" GobHob yelled.

"Can we at least wear boxes over our heads?"

GobHob slapped his head in annoyance. "Don't you think that would attract *more* attention and suspicion?"

Without any more words, they waited. What they were waiting for was unknown. Eventually, Rhino must have been bored, so he whipped out his Telecube and bit down on all sides.

***

Pierre neatly placed all the items in a large pot. Drew and Rupert watched curiously. Then Pierre reached for the mix juice.

"Uh-oh. This is an experimental brand."

"Eh. What could go wrong?" Rupert shrugged. He *really* did not want to walk all that way to the mix room.

Pierre squeezed a tiny drop of juice into the cauldron. He didn't notice the very tiny print on the bottom: "*Experimental brand warning: May cause other people to get sucked up in your spells.*"

But it was too small for anybody in the world to see. "Oh look!" Pierre exclaimed. "It says, *New! To go to certain diamond-sions, go to certain places with your diamond!*"

They all looked at the long list of diamond-sions and places where you have to be to get there.

"Where is Jimmathy?" Drew wondered. "Where did you throw him his Diamond?"

"It was a volcano in Italy. I think it was Mt. Etna," Pierre answered. He looked at the list until he found *Squooshmellow Diamond-sion, Mt. Etna, Italy.* "Jimmathy is most likely in the Squooshmellow Diamond-sion. So, we—I mean..."

Pierre paused.

"I just realised that you," he pointed to Rupert, "will be the only one who can go."

"I guess that's okay," Drew said. "I don't know if I wanna, anyway."

Suddenly, a light orange diamond floated to the top of the cauldron. It was done. Pierre quickly grabbed it and put it into his drawstring bag, which had the S.O.A.R logo printed on it.

"Let's go! To Mt. Etna we go!" He sang. Rupert and Drew followed behind.

"Great... more walking..." Rupert moaned.

"Who said we were gonna *walk*?"

"Huh?"

A land jet ski then showed up right next to them. It had the S.O.A.R logo on it.

"This land jet ski will take us to the other side of S.O.A.R in seconds!"

Pierre exclaimed.

"WHY DIDN'T WE USE THIS EAR-LIER???!!!!!!!" Rupert shouted. His feet practically shot out of his shoes.

"It only delivers TO Italian restaurants," Pierre said.

Without another word, they jumped onto the three-person-land jet ski. It was very fast—way faster than the moving sidewalk and the walking or running. They made it to where the door to the chamber and the old sheep was and walked inside. The sheep was still knitting a small bumblebee sweater.

"Hello, Pierre!" she said in sheep-ish. "Close the tile door on your way out, dearie."

They climbed into the chamber and finally made it to under table 4 of the Italian restaurant. They hustled out of there fast, but the restaurant worker yelled, "Wait! Your check!" Drew quickly signed the check, grabbed his lasagna, and then they were off.

They were lucky that Mt. Etna was close by, and with the three-person land jet ski, they made it there in less than 5 minutes.

At the exact same time, Rhino and GobHob were speeding to the Italian restaurant by the Telecube. Once they had arrived, Rhino pointed out that Rupert was now on Mt. Etna on the People-Finder. So, then they speeded to Mt. Etna by the Telecube and proceeded to walk up the volcano.

As they were walking, suddenly, Rhino disappeared with a poof, then came back one minute later.

"What the heck happened?!" GobHob screeched. "You shouldn't do that!"

"I accidentally did something

with that ol' Telecube." Rhino sputtered. "Síntoo—" He started to say something in Galician, but quickly caught himself.

"Stop talking in different languages, Martin!" GobHob shouted. "First, you're messing with the Telecube, now this? You gotta behave yourself!"

Rhino lowered his head in shame.

GobHob (who was still angry), and Rhino *finally* reached Mt. Etna, but when they stepped onto the plateau, the ground started shaking.

"Ahhhh!!" GobHob screeched, very wobbly. "An earthquake!"

Suddenly, they heard a very familiar voice and saw a swirl of orange.

"I think it's working!!" It sounded like Rupert.

"Why is it sucking us into it too?!?!" A voice that sounded like

Drew yelled.

"Baaaaa!!!" Someone bleated. It sounded like Pierre.

Luckily, GobHob was buff (for someone the size of a juvenile capybara) and grabbed to the edge of the swirl and pulled. He was still holding onto Rhino's arm, and a weird force was pulling in all directions, but, even so, Rhino and GobHob got pulled in. They were gone.

Within seconds, the orange swirl stopped. There was no sign of anyone ever being there.

And that, my friends, is how Rupert was now lost in a sea of white where gravity didn't exist. NOW we're back to present time.

Chapter 4

Philosophies, Dark Figures, and Gobble Smacks

"These items are scattered throughout the Diamond-sionverse! Dumbweed is found in the Floral dimension, Babbleapple are a fruit native to the Juice dimension, and human Lawyers are only known to exist in good old TSD." said Tahlia.

"How to get there?" asked Jimmathy.

"Well, that's the thing. We can't. It'd be less work finding the item cave and beating whoever's doing it in a big physical fight."

"Are you sure there's no other way to get to different dimensions?"

"Well... I guess no one can be absolutely sure of anything. Nothing can be certain."

"So, anything is possible?"

"Through a certain philosophy, yes."

"That means there could be another way!"

"Jimmathy, there isn't."

"But you just said there could be!"

Tahlia sighed and sat down on a Squooshmellow bench nearby. "Through a CERTAIN philosophy. Not all philosophies are true."

"Well, my photography—"

"Philosophy."

"My palaeontology is, 'We can do this!'"

Suddenly, there was a large sound nearby.

"JIMMMATHY! JIMMATHY! JIM-MATHY! JIMMATHY!"

It sounded familiar.

Rupert had meant to just go into his Diamond by himself, but Drew and Pierre had accidentally gotten sucked in, too. They had been wandering around The Squooshmellow Diamond-sion for at least a few hours of TSD time (the Squooshmellow Diamond-sion and TSD were very different time-wise).

"See? My Apology—"

"PHILOSOPHY."

"My lobotomy could work after all!"

Tahlia rolled her eyes.

"We should figure out who it is that's messing up them Diamond first before we jump to conclusions."

"Rhino. Or GobBob—sorry, Gob-Hob. Or..." Jimmathy looked around and started to sweat. "...Rupert."

Although it hurt Jimmathy to say that, no one knew exactly who Rupert was, so they assumed he was some buff sumo wrestler who was looking for revenge.

"Now that we know who it could possibly be, let's check if my phoneymosoty is right!" Jimmathy exclaimed. Tahlia sighed. Where they were walking and why they were walking was unknown, at least to Tahlia, which is probably why she asked, "Where are we going?"

Jimmathy shrugged. "I don't know. Anyway... WAIT! That rhymes!" He jumped merrily along, like it was the time of his life. He had little knowledge of rhyming. "Doo doo doodily do! Yippie doodily do! I made it to Peru!"

"We're not in Peru!" Natnat cried. "...Wait. Are we?"

"No," Tahlia said with a sigh.

"Deedily dee hooray! I made it to Uruguay!"

"Ooh, Uruguay!" said Gideon. "It's

that little lobe-shaped country on the edge of Sloth Ameareca, right?"

"Eh... sure," said Tahlia. She had had a lot of time to explain all about Earth to the Squooshmellows, but sometimes they got a bit confused.

"Scorch Eggplantia! I remember! Azbadom Ranfroost and all that?"

"Actually..."

There were thirty more minutes of explaining the geographical position and properties of various Earth continents, including, but not limited to, North America, South America, Africa, Europe, Asia, Oceania, and Antarctica. What does that leave, you ask? Zealandia. Look it up. After explaining the precise size and shape of Hudson Bay, the exact number of islands in Indonesia, and the extreme disproportionalities that result from certain map projections through trying to map a spherical planet in a rectangular frame which forces the landmasses at the top and bottom to stretch out and appear larger than they are in reality, Thalia got tired and got everyone back on track.

"We can discuss Earth geography later. Let's keep moving," she said.

"Moving where?" asked Jimmathy.

"WHAT!?!? Thalia exclaimed. I thought you were leading the way!"

"While you were talking, I forgot."

"Ok... well...."

"HOLLY NUTCRACKERS!" Jimmathy yelled, "IT'S RUPERT, PIERRE, AND DREW!"

Everyone turned to look where Jimmathy was pointing. Sure enough, Rupert, Pierre, and Drew were marching merrily along as they talked, laughed, and hoped

Jimmathy was there. He was.

"RUPERT!" Jimmathy yelled. "Over here!"

Rupert looked over and immediately ran over, a beam on his face.

"Jimmathy!"

Really happy music played. But on the side of a hill out in the distance, a shadowy figure was spying on them from afar (hint: The figure's name starts with G and rhymes with *SchmobHob*). The music got dark and dramatic.

"The music is dark and dramatic! This can't be good!" Drew panicked.

Still, Rupert did not stop until he reached Jimmathy and gave him a big hug. The rest of the group tried to figure out why the music was so dark and dramatic.

"I think it's something in C# minor. Very dark and dramatic," said Thalia.

"Definitely," agreed Drew.

"The only reason this sort of music would play was if something truly ominous was happening," said Rolnalda.

"Baaaaaaaa Baa Ba baaaaa baaa Ba baaaa Ba ba Baaaaaa baaaaaaaaa Ba baa Baaa ba," said Pierre, which meant, "*Let's secure the area.*"

"Agreed!" said everyone in unison. They all went in different directions.

In time they all began to notice the figure, then came straight back.

The figure left.

Meanwhile, Jimmathy was telling everything that had happened. Rupert had told Jimmathy everything that had happened.

"Pierre and Drew helped—"

"Squooshmellow friends—"

"Made my own Diamond—"

"Volcano gobbled me up—"

"Jimmathy!"

"Rupert!"

Jimmathy hesitated and looked the way where the figure once was. "You're gonna get us out of here, right?"

Rupert sat down and sighed. He couldn't even gasp at how soft the ground was. HOW did he suck Drew and Pierre into his Diamond? WHO was the figure in the shadows? WHY did he take GobHob's place at WAGGA? The question hung deep in Rupert's chest, turning every feeling he felt into guilt, but also despair. The Squooshmellows, Drew, Tahlia, and Pierre ran over.

"I don't know who that figure was, but he's definitely not from around here!" Rolnalda yelled.

"How do you know?" Drew asked.

"Because everyone from around here is happy and fun and delighted

24/7! They don't loom in the shadows, eavesdropping... without saying hello."

"I know who it is!" Tahlia exclaimed.

"Who?!" Everyone else exclaimed back. They knew that soon they're problems would be over....

"*The person who is messing with Jimmathy's Diamond*!" Tahlia said as if it was obvious.

"I THOUGHT YOU KNEW *WHO*!" Jimmathy yelled. "That's just a *what*."

The Squooshmellows nodded and crossed their arms at Tahlia. Rupert, Drew, and Pierre tilted their heads.

"What's this about someone messing with Jimmathy's Diamond?" Rupert asked.

"I lost my Diamond, but then later

I totally went berserk, and we figured out that someone was messing with my Diamond!" Jimmathy explained.

"Well, then, it has to be Rhino or GobHob! Or Rhino *and* GobHob. Who else could it be?" said Rupert.

"Then we should find this figure!" Drew exclaimed. "We're a large group. Let's introduce, shall we? I'm Drew, this is Pierre, and Rupert. We're all friends of Jimmathy and are from TSD."

"I'm Tahlia! I'm originally from TSD, too, but live here now. These are all my Squooshmellow friends: Rolnalda, who's the yeti, Natnat is the alien, Sawtelle is the pancakes. Finally, there is Austin, the avocado... and also Gideon, the guacamole, is on the other side."

"7... 8... 9... We have 9 people. 10 different brains. That's a lot! We should split up." Rupert stated. "I want Pierre and Drew to go up to Pancake Hills. Tahlia and Sawtelle, to the Squooshforest. Austin and Gideon, to the Fabric Meadow. Natnat and Rolnalda over to that stream of stuffing. Finally, Jimmathy and I will go over to that abandoned wooden house labelled 'RhiHob— STAY OUT!!!' Before you all go, if you find anything, yodel, 'GOBBLE SMACK!!!'"

Everyone nodded and split up (again).

Jimmathy and Rupert ran over to the abandoned house as fast as they could (am I getting "*run, run, as fast as you can, you can't catch me I'm the gingerbread man*" vibes here)?

It was made entirely of wood, which was awfully suspicious since no wood was *anywhere*. Everything was made of Squooshellow. Even the trees were made of soft fabric and stuffing and looked as though they could bend over any second! Jimmathy and Rupert weren't even sure how the people who built it got the wood and nails in the first place.

Once they reached the old house, Rupert paused and looked at Jimmathy, confused. "RhiHob sounds familiar. Where have I heard it before?" Rupert wondered, tapping his chin and gazing up at the sign.

"You're right!" exclaimed Jimmathy. "'Hob' sounds familiar. Oh yeah! The craft and home decor store, Hobby Bobby!"

Rupert nodded. "That's true, but I was thinking about something else. You know, I just went to that store when I was decorating my new office..." Rupert's voice trailed off. He paused and looked at his feet.

"I didn't think that WAGGA goblins got offices, did they?" Jimmathy asked.

Rupert looked up. "So, you *aren't* mad about the whole job thing?"

"Oh, yes, I am. But still, it's great and all that you get to have your job back and stuff. When I got blasted off into a different dimension, I realised how much I missed you. I guess I'm not *that* mad anymore." Jimmathy confessed.

"Great..." Rupert muttered, "because I need to tell you something, and you might lose your marbles."

"What?!"

"GobHob retired..."

"That's great news!"

"...And he told me to take his place as WAGGA World Professor."

Suddenly, five marbles fell out of Jimmathy's pocket and landed on

the soft ground, instantly disappear-
ing into the soft abyss.

"My marbles!" Jimmathy wailed.

Rupert waited. Then he figured
that it would be better to just open
the wooden door and not wait for
Jimmathy's next response.

On closer inspection of the door,
there was a smaller print on the sign
which read, "Not a secret base." Rupert stopped, looked around, but
then turned the knob of the door
and peered inside, ready for something to pounce.

It was dusty in there, and it
smelled like the wood was rotting.
Jimmathy walked inside, his eyes
wide. They couldn't *really* see anything, but when they heard a small
voice and some heavy breathing,
they could finally see a large figure
sitting at a table. The table seemed
too tiny for him.

"Anda tidak sepatutnya berbuat demikian," the voice said.

It was Rhino. And he was speaking in Malay.

Rupert grabbed his *Foreign Language Translator Headwear LXXIV* from his pocket.

Jimmathy looked at Rhino, and Rhino cracked his knuckles.

"Well, well, well. What do we have here?" Rhino asked in Chinese.

"Run!" Rupert yelled. Jimmathy and Rupert bolted out of the wooden house.

Meanwhile, GobHob was enjoying his new life as an author. His new book (titled "GobHob") was the one he just started.

"*I waited at the door, my father's foot tapping on the loose wood. His stern face made me stand up straighter, but he... but he....*" GobHob was stuck. No ideas. He punched his typewriter and his papers—along with the keys to the typewriter—went flying around his office.

"...GobHob?" A small voice outside his room said.

"Go away..." GobHob responded, "I'm not GobHob anymore."

"...But... What about RhiHob?" The voice said.

"...Martin?" GobHob said. Rhino opened the door and smiled. GobHob slowly walked towards Rhino and hugged him.

"OW! Your horn poked me!" GobHob yelped. Rhino ignored GobHob, but he backed away. It was best to keep a distance from GobHob when he was mad.

"Uh... GobHob?"

"Um... Yes, Martin?" GobHob asked.

"I just saw... Jimmathy and Rupert."

"I know. I saw them, too." GobHob mumbled. "We're in trouble."

"No, we're not!" Rhino yelled, slamming his hands on the table. "Listen: We grab Rupert and Jimmathy and go. We throw them into a pit, or *anything*."

GobHob seemed to consider this. "Yes, but they always seem to find a way to crawl back. We need a way to *really* get rid of them."

Rhino nodded. "Yes! I know how." GobHob brightened. He started picking up the things he had dropped on the floor. Rhino smiled evilly.

"It all starts with my herd, Bob-Gob, ...and those Squooshmellow friends of theirs."

Chapter 5

Tele-monds, Jorts, and Proper Licencing

Jimmathy and Rupert ran as fast as they could while yelling, "GOBBLE, SMACK!!!".

"*How* did Rhino get into this Diamond-sion?!" Jimmathy asked once they came to a stop.

"...No idea, actually. But I'm pretty sure it has something to do with how I accidentally sucked Drew and Pierre into my Diamond, too," Rupert replied, brushing off loose Squooshmellow stuffing off his toilet paper trousers.

Suddenly, there was shouting: "*We're coming!!!!!!!*" It was Rolnalda, Sawtelle, Natnat, Gideon & Austin, Drew, Tahlia, and Pierre. They had all come running from where they had just been sent to.

"Rhino!" said Jimmathy.

"Shack!!" Followed by Rupert.

"Problem!!!" They said in unison. "RHINO SHACK PROBLEM!!!!!" They said with many exclamation points.

"A RHINO SHACK PROBLEM!?!?" Drew was stunned. "THAT'S THE WORST TYPE OF PACHYDERM BUILDING OCCURRENCE RIGHT AFTER ELEPHANT WAREHOUSE IN-CIDENT AND HIPPOPOTAMUS SHOE SHOP EMERGENCY!!!"

"I KNOW!!!" Jimmathy said fright-fully. "But we have to stay calm!"

"Or there won't be any calm left to stay," Rupert added.

Abruptly, Jimmathy started to climb a tree for some reason and did jumping jacks. Steam came out of his ears.

"*Oh, I was walking in Panama,*

feeling kind of sweaty,

I met a ship captain, who was big as a yeti,

He offered me a nice big bowl of spaghetti,

But he was really Rhino so away I did get-y!

Oh, no, no, no. don't go on that ship!

Oh nein, nein, nein. He'll eat you like a chip!

So steer clear. Save yourself the trip!

Because he's really Rhino, so don't go on that ship!"

"He's singing again!" Natnat exclaimed.

"We must be close." Gideon noted.

"Should we... go together?" Thalia said. "I mean, if Rhino's here, then he's probably the one messing with Jimmathy."

Everyone looked at the shack. Then at Jimmathy and Rupert. Then at Pierre for some reason. They looked up, down, down, left, up, right, down, up, right, up, down, left. (This is coincidentally also the cheat code for beating the level 2 boss of Jimmathy's favourite video game, Holy Kannoli 4.)

Eventually, they all agreed.

The shack was, in all of its shack-ness, very shack-y. Rupert opened the door of the shack-y shack, and Rupert, Drew, and Pierre gasped. (Jimmathy was too busy examining his pointy shoes to notice.)

They gasped at GobHob, sitting next to Rhino. A typewriter without keys was set on the table, along with a pile of typewriter keys and loose papers.

"GobHob is here, too!" Everybody exclaimed. (The Squooshmellows were pretty lost, although they assumed GobHob was Rhino's partner.)

GobHob slammed his hands on the table, and all the typewriter keys went flying (again).

"YOU!" Jimmathy yelled. It seemed as though he was out of the trance, until...

"*GobHob,*

SmogeHob

BobHob

HobGob

Stay away

Or you will pay

Oh... GobHob

BobHob

Today is the day...!" Jimmathy continued the song, but luckily Rupert managed to cover Jimmathy's mouth, and he stopped singing. Out of the corner of Rupert's eye, he saw GobHob and Rhino look at each other evilly. Rupert knew something was coming. And it would be bad. Possibly this would be the end.

GobHob held up Jimmathy's diamond.

"Искате ли тази?" Rhino asked teasingly.

GobHob glared at Rhino.

"Erm, I mean... Do you want this?"

"Um... Yes, actually. We do." said Rupert.

"Nuh uh uh. We've grown quite fond of the thing. It's so... *Sparkly*," GobHob said in a harsh whisper.

"What tricks are you planning!?" said Thalia.

Rhino chuckled.

"Lots."

Rupert lunged at Rhino, but Rhino was quick and stepped out of the way. Tahlia was next, and ran towards Rhino too, but Rhino just picked Tahlia up, as if she was as light as a feather. Tahlia squirmed and kicked, but Rhino still held strong.

The Squooshmellows formed a huddle and whispered together, then put their hands in the middle and yelled, "GO! GO SQOOSHLAND!"

It was time for their plan to come into action. They circled Rhino suspiciously, then pounced, toppling Rhino to the floor. Tahlia scrambled out of Rhino's grip, and at the same time, Rupert attempted to grab Jimmathy's Diamond from GobHob. Drew and Pierre tried to pry the diamond out of GobHob's hands. It was pretty easy, given his size. Pierre handed it to Rupert, and Rupert handed it to Jimmathy. Jimmathy raced out the door with his Diamond and hid in a Squoosh-bush.

Meanwhile, the Squooshmellows were still trying to keep Rhino pinned down. Rupert did the math in his head. Rhino was about 2,000 pounds. The Squooshmellows were very light, even though there were 5 or 6 (whether or not you count Gideon and Austin as 1 or 2) of them. They were each a pound, and that was not even a quarter of Rhino's body weight. However, Rupert also had another problem. Drew and Pierre were struggling to keep Gob-Hob to stay down. Even though they were twice his size, GobHob was wiggly and easily slipped out of their grip. Rupert had an idea. He spotted some rope in a corner.

"Tie them up!" Rupert grabbed the rope and threw it to the Squooshmellows, who tied up Rhino like a burrito. Then they quickly focused their attention on GobHob. He was weeping; for Rupert had taken away his most prized possession—his WAGGA pin labelled "GobHob of WAG." He was even listening to "*The Happy Song*," which was his happy song. He only listened to that if he was *really* sad, like now. He was also weeping because his BFF, Rhino (they had literally made friendship bracelets), was tied up. Finally, he was also crying because Jimmathy had gotten away, and he knew that he was going to get tied up too. But that didn't stop anybody. They wrapped the scratchy rope around GobHob's limp body and attached it to Rhino.

GobHob's sadness drained away almost instantly. Now he felt despair and madness. He was going to use that rope to tie up Jimmathy, not the other way around.

As soon as Rolnalda, Natnat, Sawtelle, Gideon, Austin, Tahlia, Drew, Pierre, and Rupert were sure that

GobHob and Rhino were secure, they bolted out of the wooden house to Jimmathy. Jimmathy was curled up in a ball, shaking.

"Gee, what's wrong?" asked Rupert.

"Whenever I get the hiccups, my whole body shakes," replied Jimmathy. He rolled onto his belly when, *crack!* Everybody froze. Jimmathy rolled over to see what had broken. Everybody gasped when they saw that it was, in fact, Jimmathy's Diamond. Time seemed to stop. Everybody was just looking at the many pieces of blue diamond.

"How am I gonna get home?!" Jimmathy wailed.

"How am *I* gonna get home?" Said Drew.

"Ba baa *ba* baaa baa baa baa?" Pierre asked.

Rupert sighed, scooped up the

pieces, and put them in his WAGGA satchel. Then his eyes lit up.

"What is it?" Drew asked.

"I have my Diamond!" Rupert replied, pulling out a smaller Diamond.

"Yeah, thanks for rubbing it in. You can go home, but *we're* stuck here forever."

"No!" Rupert exclaimed. "Listen! *How* did you get here?"

Pierre and Drew thought for a second. "We travelled from your Diamond. But how?" Drew scratched his chin.

"It's easy! We didn't go to the Mix Room, we went to the Mix Chamber! And with that mix glop or whatever, it was an experimental brand. It changed my Diamond! We can suck up *everybody* back."

Pierre nodded. "Baaa!" Which meant, "Yes, I think you're right!"

"We *WILL* get home!" Jimmathy yelled, smiling. Rupert was happy too, but he was also wondering what would happen when he would be officially head of WAGGA. (He was an intern at that time).

"But what about GobHob and Rhino?" Drew asked. "They're gonna escape somehow."

Jimmathy thought about it for a second. "What if we use something that blasts *different* people into a di-amond-sion in seconds, and they can't get out!"

"So, like basically a Telecube, Dia-mond?" Drew asked. Jimmathy nodded. "Yes! In fact, this is a newly discovered form of travelling to dia-mond-sions. It's called a Tele-mond! Basically, it works as both a Tele-cube, *and* a Diamond. It makes someone go to a random place in a random dimension, *and* you can't get out!" Drew said.

Pierre started connecting the dots. "I've heard of this, I think. Since it is kind of the exact opposite, don't you combine your three *least* favourite items together? And then BOOM! Right?" (Rupert had to translate with his new skill, Sheepish.)

"It makes sense," Tahlia said. Everyone gasped; they had forgotten that she and the Squooshmellows were there, too.

"What if we make one of those and use it on GobHob and Rhino, will that work?" Jimmathy asked.

"JIMMATHY YOU GENIUS!" Rupert exclaimed.

"Technically, it's against the TSD Department of Telecommunications, but who cares! We're not in TSD!" Pierre said. Everyone cheered.

"But we would have to go to

S.O.A.R, Sheep Obey all Rules, to make it. I'm guessing that there is no S.O.A.R HQ here?" Rupert asked.

"Erm, actually...," Pierre said, "there is. Deep, deep underground. You have to be a S.O.A.R HQ agent with 5 years of experience to get in, though. Luckily, I'm a S.O.A.R HQ agent with 5 years of experience. Let's go!"

"Lead the way!" Jimmathy exclaimed.

"Hold up." Said Tahlia. "A few of us should stay behind with Rhino and GobGob—"

"Gob*Hob*," Jimmathy corrected.

"And I can do it." Tahlia finished. The Squooshmellows offered too.

"Great!" Drew exclaimed. "We'll come find you once we're done."

***

Jimmathy, Rupert, Drew (he was just there for translating purposes only), and Pierre were finally there. In the S.O.A.R HQ lobby, Pierre was greeted by an old-man-sheep. He directed the party to the room full of squares, where they would get Jimmathy's least favourite items. Thankfully, the room was just down the hall (and the hall was 5 miles long). Once they were there, Drew asked Jimmathy personal information into the computer.

"Full name?"

"Jimmathy Jimmathy Davis."

"Your middle name is Jimmathy, too?"

"Uh, yeah. Isn't everybody's?" Everybody shrugged.

"Birthday?"

"August Ninth, 2007."

"Phone number?"

"What?! I don't know!"

"Okay... Do you have an email?"

"I only know of mail without an E in the front."

"Alright, skipping that question. Do you know your address?"

"Uh... I think it was 2468 Skatepark Lane, Townville City, NR or Notorado."

Drew typed on the computer. But before he hit send, he asked,

"Now, what do you *think* are your three least favourite non-living items, Jimmathy?"

"Well, I hate jorts, smelly markers, and *Harry Potter* books," Jimmathy said.

"What are jorts?" Pierre asked. Drew translated.

Jimmathy replied, "jorts are jean shorts. Ick."

Drew hit send and suddenly, a pair of jorts, a grape smelly marker, and the 2nd *Harry Potter* book appeared out of an old and rusty pipe. Pierre grabbed them and they ran back to the old-man-sheep. Pierre asked for directions to the Tele-mond Mix Room. It just so happened that it was just that they had come from 2 miles down the hall. Everybody groaned.

Soon everyone was in the Mix Room, making a Tele-mond for Jimmathy.

Pierre put Jimmathy's items in the cauldron. Then he poured in the tan glop. Luckily, it wasn't an experimental brand. Soon, as usual, a shape popped up in the tan liquid. This time it was a medium-sized tan-ish gold circle. All that sudden, an angelic choir started singing "*Joy to the World.*"

"What's that noise?" Jimmathy asked.

"The celebration noise! Silly!" Rupert said.

"Whenever someone makes a newly-discovered thing, it plays through the new epic surround-sound speakers!" Pierre said in Sheepish. Drew and Rupert forgot to translate and Jimmathy had no clue what Pierre said.

"You should really learn Sheepish, Jimmathy! It's pretty easy! You should use Duobingo. That's how I learned Sheepish in only *TWO DAYS*!" Rupert said.

Jimmathy thought about it. Finally, Jimmathy replied, "May I see your phone?"

As promised, in 2 days, Jimmathy was fluent in Sheepish. He also had a working Tele-mond! (They had spent their 2 days travelling back to the shack.)

"Let's fire up this tloo-mind and

split!" Jimmathy said.

"Hold up. First, you need a Squooshland Department of Tele-communications Tele-mond Licence," Rupert said.

Jimmathy ran towards the shack. Everyone just ran with him.

"Why are we running to the shack?" Everyone said.

"WE'RE GOING TO BLAST RHINO AND GOBHOB TO A RANDOM PLACE IN A RANDOM DIAMOND-SION WITH THIS BAD BOY!" Jimmathy exclaimed as he pointed to his Tele-mond.

"Slow down, you don't have a licence, *and* you don't know how it works!" Rupert said.

"I DON'T CARE! I'M LIVING LIFE FREELY NOW!" Jimmathy said.

Drew and Pierre hung behind Rupert and Jimmathy. They wanted *Rupert* to stop Jimmathy.

"You'll get arrested by the universe police!" Rupert yelled.

"UGH! Fine, I'll get a licence."

So, he went to the Squooshland Department of Telecommunications, waited in line for about forty-five minutes, filled out the form, then got his picture taken. They had to keep retaking his picture, as he seemed to always blink the moment a photo was taken. (They had to trick his eyes with a picture of ice cream.). Then Jimmathy came trousering back with his new Tele-mond licence.

"There, you happy now? It's valid for the next five years."

Drew, Pierre, and Rupert were napping. Jimmathy tapped Rupert on the shoulder. Rupert sighed, his eyes half closed, and gave a thumbs up. He woke up Drew and Pierre. (For Pierre it took a lot longer since

Pierre is such a sound sleeper.) They also reluctantly gave Jimmathy the green flag. Jimmathy marched into the old shack and saw Rhino and GobHob also sleeping.

"Why are you sleeping? It's paradoxically not dark out!" Jimmathy said, waking both Rhino and Gob-Hob.

"First of all, in Squooshland it doesn't get dark, but it is nighttime. Second of all, WHAT ARE YOU DO-ING HERE!?!?" GobHob exclaimed.

"Jimmathy," Rhino said, quickly jerking into an upright position, "you monster."

Rupert started to walk towards the shack to help Jimmathy, but Jimmathy stopped Rupert.

"Don't worry... I can do this on my own."

Rupert backed away slowly. "Bu-tyoumustlistentomebecausethe-

Tele-mondisreallydangerousand-
youneedtoknowhowtooperate-"

"I can do this on my own!" Jimmathy yelled again. There was a
crackle of thunder (or possibly just
Rhino's cough), and a flash of light-
ning. (Possibly just the glitter of
Rhino's gold teeth.) Then it started
raining. (Possibly just Rhino's sweat
dripping down.)

Rupert frowned. "FINE!" And he
wandered out of the shack.

"Oh no! It's raining! This shack
doesn't have a roof! We'll get
soaked!" Tahlia said from inside the
shack.

"Tahlia...?" Jimmathy said.

"I've been here this whole time.
Squooshmellows, too," said Tahlia.

"...Oh," said Jimmathy.

"It is raining!" Rupert said from a
distance.

Jimmathy examined the Tele-mond. It was a small tan sphere, with three silver buttons on the side. (Of course, a sphere does not have *sides* because the entire surface is bowed at a perfect curve.) Jimmathy tried to read what the buttons said, but he couldn't read. He squinted at the words:

"*Diamond*"

"*Telecube*"

"*Tele-mond*"

The Diamond button would work like a Diamond. The Telecube button would work like a Telecube. And the Tele-mond would work like a— you guessed it—a *banana*! (JK!) The Tele-mond button would work like a Tele-mond. Simple common sense.

"Press the Telemond one. That's the bottom one," said Pierre, "and whisper GobHob and Rhino's *real* names. Okay?"

"Wait, you're here, too?" Jimmathy said.

"Yeah..." Pierre said.

"Oh," Jimmathy responded.

Jimmathy then nodded. He crossed his fingers, threw some salt behind his back (it hit Tahlia in the face), and pressed the *"Tele-mond"* button. Jimmathy whispered, "Gob-Hob, Martin / Rhino." ...And then it happened.

From the outside of the shack, you would see a HUGE flash of purple, dark blue, and tan. Those were Jimmathy's 3 least favourite colours.

Suddenly, Rhino and GobHob got blurry. Then they appeared to spin around, until they were gone.

After GobHob and Rhino were in "Fireland," Jimmathy rubbed his hands together in the cold rain.

"What happened? Where are GobHob and Rhino?" Thalia asked.

Jimmathy merely replied, "Gone." And then curled up and went to sleep. And the only sounds that could be heard were the pitter-patter of heavy rain and the gentle rumble of thunder in the distance.

The next morning, after a yummy breakfast at Tahlia's house and a short wander around the beautiful Diamond-sion (it's even more pretty after it rains), Jimmathy, Rupert, and Pierre stood in a line. Rupert held his Diamond in his left hand.

"Ready?" Rupert asked.

Drew and Tahlia waited for their response. Drew loved it in the Squooshmellow Diamond-sion and decided to stay. Tahlia—even though the whole point was to go back to TSD, decided to stay, too. She loved it in Squooshmellow Diamond-sion. Besides, she still had the Squooshmellows, and now Drew to keep her company.

"Goodbye," Drew said to Pierre, holding back tears.

"Goodbye," Tahlia said, waving. "Come visit sometime!"

"BYE!" everyone said to Drew and Tahlia.

"So, how do we get back, anyway?" Rupert asked.

"Hold it in your hands and whisper, 'TSD' three times into your Diamond." Pierre replied. Jimmathy was glad he could finally understand Sheepish.

"Don't worry, it only works for getting back. I promise, it wasn't *that* easy."

Rupert nodded, whispered, and there was a bright flash of light. Pierre, Rupert, and Jimmathy were gone.

***

GobHob, after climbing out of a ditch, reached the top.

"Finally! I've found a way to escape!" Rhino stood beside him.

The small flicker of light from his candle burnt out as he blew it out. GobHob stood up, dusted off his knees, and blew his nose on a handkerchief. He placed the handkerchief back in his pocket and scanned the sky. It seemed to be clear.

Suddenly, a huge eagle swooped down and carried them to the sky. GobHob and Rhino were gone.

HOW will Rupert organise and keep WAGGA safe?

WILL anyone use that Tele-mond again?

ARE GobHob and Rhino for sure gone?

Find out in:

JIMMATHY'S ODYSSEY 4

A Tale of Definite Heroes

About the Authors

Isaac, Violet, Simon, and Elsie are students. They love writing about Jimmathy and creating funny characters. They all enjoy writing humorous books together. *Jimmathy's Odyssey III* is their third book they've ever published. Isaac enjoys DJing, Simon likes mustard, Violet likes Disney, and Elsie likes musicals a bit too much.

9 798888 704370